This book belongs to:

_____

This paperback edition first published in 2009 by Andersen Press Ltd.,
20 Vauxhall Bridge Road, London SW1V 2SA.
First published in Great Britain in 1969 by Blackie.
Published in Australia by Random House Australia Pty.,
Level 3, 100 Pacific Highway, North Sydney, NSW 2060.
Text copyright © John Yeoman, 1969.
Illustration copyright © Quentin Blake, 1969.
The rights of John Yeoman and Quentin Blake to be identified as the
author and illustrator of this work have been asserted by them in
accordance with the Copyright, Designs and Patents Act, 1988.
All rights reserved. Colour separated in Switzerland by Photolitho AG, Zürich.
Printed and bound in Singapore by Tien Wah Press.

10 9 8 7 6 5 4 3

British Library Cataloguing in Publication Data available.

ISBN 978 1 84270 916 0

This book has been printed on acid-free paper

The Bear's Winter House

John Yeoman   Quentin Blake

ANDERSEN PRESS

One chilly day at the very end of summer the hen found the squirrel, the hedgehog and the pig peeping at something through the bushes. "What are you looking at?" she asked them.

"We're looking at the bear," said the hedgehog.
"He's behaving in a very strange way," said the squirrel.
"Climb on my back and have a look," said the pig.
So the hen fluttered up on to the pig's back.
And there, through the bushes, she could see the bear running off into the woods and returning with armfuls of large branches and logs.
"But that isn't all," said the squirrel.

And it wasn't. For then the hen saw the bear scrape up some soft moss from the ground and put it in a neat pile. Dying to know what was happening, they all moved forward. But the bear did not notice them because he was so busy picking up his logs and banging them into the ground.

"Hmm, hmm," said the hedgehog. "What are you doing, bear?"
But the bear only hummed to himself and began to weave some branches between the big logs.

"What are you doing, bear?" grunted the pig, loudly.
The bear noticed them and said, "Every winter when I
am supposed to be asleep I lie awake shivering. But this
winter will be different. Look at this piece of paper."
The animals crowded round the paper and the bear
told them that it was a plan for a winter house.
"I am building it with good strong logs and branches,
and moss to keep out the wind," he said. "And if you
help me you can share my winter house."

The other animals all laughed at this and said that the bear was silly. But the bear took no notice of them and began to fill up the cracks with moss. "We shall see who sleeps well when winter comes," he said.

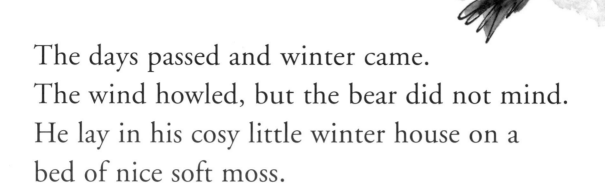

The days passed and winter came.
The wind howled, but the bear did not mind.
He lay in his cosy little winter house on a
bed of nice soft moss.

But the squirrel, who usually spends the winter asleep
in a nest of loose twigs at the top of a tall tree, was
unhappy. The branches swayed this way and that
in the wind, and nearly threw the poor squirrel
out of bed.

And the hedgehog, who usually rolls
himself up in a ball among the leaves in
winter, was unhappy at the foot of the
tall tree. Although he had curled himself
up into a tight ball, the damp leaves
would not stick to him because the gale
swept them all away.

And the pig was unhappy in his sty.
The icy wind had blown away all his straw and left
him shivering on the cold stone floor.

And the hen was unhappy on her
perch because the strong wind
blew through all the cracks in the
hen-house and made her sneeze.

At last the four animals could
stand it no longer. They all walked
sadly through the wind and rain to
the bear's winter house and begged
him to let them in.

As he was a very kind bear he got up from his cosy bed of moss and made a small hole in the wall for them to squeeze through. He didn't even say, "I told you so!" The squirrel, the pig, the hedgehog and the hen all thanked the bear and helped him to fill up the hole in the wall again. And when that was done the bear gave them all some of his moss bed and said, "Now let's all have a nice long winter sleep."

But the other animals were too warm and happy to sleep. "Let's have a party!" they cried. The bear tried to tell them that the little house was too small, but they wouldn't listen. First the pig made them play 'Hunt the honeycomb'.

And when they had turned the place upside-down looking for the honeycomb (which was in the bear's bed), the hen got them all to sing songs. The poor bear tried to sleep, but there was far too much noise.

After that the squirrel wanted to dance.
The pig was so fat that he made the walls shake, and the
hen kept perching on the bear's head and slipping down.
What is more, the squirrel's tail kept brushing the bear's
nose and the hedgehog would keep getting under his
feet. The little house was much too small for a party.

After all that they made the poor bear play
Blind Man's Buff all through October and
November and December and January and
February – in fact, until March.

Then they all put their heads out of doors and saw that it was a wonderful spring morning.

"Goodbye, bear," they called. "And thank you. We'll be back again next winter."

But as soon as the squirrel and the pig and the hedgehog
and the hen had all gone, the bear took his little winter
house to bits and, with his arms full of logs, branches
and moss, he tiptoed to the other end of the forest.
And there, out of sight of all the other animals, he built
his little house again and snuggled down cosily in
the soft moss. "I think I need another forty
winks," he said drowsily, as he closed his eyes.
And I don't blame him, do you?

Also by Quentin Blake